LOONEY TUNES
BACK IN ACTION™

JOKE BOOK

Check out these other
Looney Tunes: Back in Action
titles from Scholastic!

Looney Tunes: Back in Action Junior Novelization
Adapted by Jenny Markas

Looney Tunes Movie Storybook
Adapted by Jane Mason

LOONEY TUNES

BACK IN ACTION™

JOKE BOOK

By Jesse Leon McCann

SCHOLASTIC INC.

NEW YORK   TORONTO   LONDON   AUCKLAND   SYDNEY
MEXICO CITY   NEW DELHI   HONG KONG   BUENOS AIRES

No part of this publication may be
reproduced in whole or in part, or stored in a
retrieval system, or transmitted in any form or by
any means, electronic, mechanical, photocopying,
recording, or otherwise, without written permission of
the publisher. For information regarding permission, write
to Scholastic Inc., Attention: Permissions Department, 557
Broadway, New York, NY 10012.
ISBN 0-439-52138-6

Cover design by Glenn Davis
Interior design by Bethany Dixon

12 11 10 9 8 7 6 5 4 3 2 1   3 4 5 6 7 8/0
Printed in the U.S.A.
First printing, September 2003

LOONEY TUNES

BACK IN ACTION™

JOKE BOOK

GRANNY: My Sylvester isn't well. Do you know a good animal doctor?

BUGS: No, all the doctors I know are people!

Q. What do you call Daffy Duck when he's holding a stick of dynamite?

A. A fire*quacker*!

Q. What do you give Tweety when he's feeling sick?

A. Medical *tweet*ment.

Q. What do you call it when Sylvester gets into a bad accident?

A. A *cat*astrophe!

1

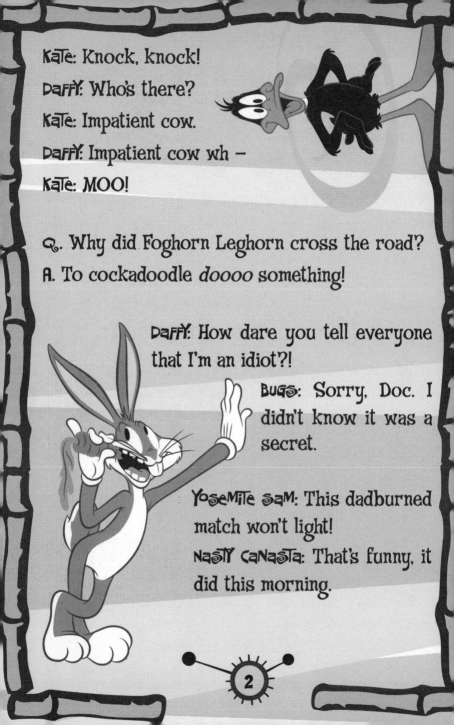

KATE: Knock, knock!

DAFFY: Who's there?

KATE: Impatient cow.

DAFFY: Impatient cow wh –

KATE: MOO!

Q. Why did Foghorn Leghorn cross the road?

A. To cockadoodle *doooo* something!

DAFFY: How dare you tell everyone that I'm an idiot?!

BUGS: Sorry, Doc. I didn't know it was a secret.

YOSEMITE SAM: This dadburned match won't light!

NASTY CANASTA: That's funny, it did this morning.

DJ: What steps would you take if the Tasmanian Devil was chasing you?

BUGS: Big ones!

Q. Where did Bugs learn to fly a rocket spy car?

A. In the *hare* force.

DAFFY: Stop! You're driving the wrong way down a one-way street!

DJ: Yeah, but I'm only going one way.

KATE: Eeek! We're going to hit that wall!

BUGS: And I'll never get over it.

Q. What goes "Moooooz"?

A. A rocket spy car going backward.

Q. What kind of doctor did Daffy see after his car hit a wall?

A. A quack!

Q. Why does Foghorn Leghorn watch TV?

A. For *hen*tertainment!

BUGS: Did you hear what happened when Yosemite Sam put dynamite in his fridge?

DAFFY: What happened?

BUGS: He blew his cool!

Bugs: I've got a wonder watch. It only cost fifty cents.

Kate: Why is it a wonder watch?

Bugs: Because every time I look at it, I wonder if it's still working!

DJ: Quick, take the wheel!

Daffy: Why?

DJ: Because there's a tree coming straight for us!

MR. Warner: Remember, success comes before work!

Kate: Where does success come before work?

MR. Warner: In the dictionary!

Q. Why did the silly alien monster stand on his head?

A. His feet were tired!

KATE: What is the best thing to take into the desert?

BUGS: A thirst-aid kit!

YOSEMITE SAM: Is heading to Las Vegas the quickest way to double your money?

DUSTY TAILS: No, the quickest way is to fold it in half!

Q. What kind of programs does Daffy watch on TV?

A. *Duck*umentaries!

Q. What does Daffy say when he's finished shopping?

A. "Put it on my bill, please."

Q. What would Sylvester get if he ran over Tweety with a lawn mower?

A. Shredded Tweet!

DJ: They should have named you Laryngitis Duck.

DAFFY: Why?

DJ: You're such a pain in the neck!

YOSEMITE SAM: I wish I had a pair of alligator shoes.

NASTY CANASTA: What size shoe does your alligator wear?

KATE: What kind of things does Taz eat?

BUGS: He eats anything he can find.

KATE: What if he can't find anything?

BUGS: Then he'll eat something else!

DUSTY TAILS: You're cute, but your legs are too short.

YOSEMITE SAM: What in tarnation are ya talkin' about? Both of them reach the floor!

Q. What's the best way to get Bugs' attention?
A. Make a noise like a carrot!

DAFFY: Darn! Try as I might, I couldn't trick that spoilsport Porky into the pit I dug!

BUGS: Well, you know what they say, Doc. It's hard to fit a square pig into a round hole.

Q. Where does Porky keep his allowance money?
A. In a piggy bank!

DaMiaN DRaKe: If you want to be a superspy, you must be able to dress for formal occasions.

DaFFY: Don't worry, pal. I've got a *duxedo!*

Q. What's left in the tub after Daffy takes a bath?

A. Fowl water.

KaTe: If you're so smart, tell me something I don't know.

DJ: Okay. There's dirt on the end of your nose.

YoseMiTe SaM: I think we better put our beds in the basement, boys.

CoTTONTaiL SMiTH: Why, boss?

YoseMiTe SaM: We gotta lay low for a while!

Q. What happened when Pepe Le Pew flew in a hot-air balloon?

A. He raised a stink!

DAFFY: I hate the pine trees in this forest!

BUGS: Why, Doc?

DAFFY: They're always needling me!

BUGS: I believe I'm being followed!

KATE: What makes you say that?

BUGS: I've got a tail on me, haven't I?

DAFFY: I'm a lucky duck! I found a four-leaf clover!

BUGS: That's nothin', Doc. I've got four rabbit's feet!

Q. What does Pepe Le Pew put on his vegetables?
A. Smelling salts!

DJ: There's not a drop of water in this entire desert.
Daffy: That's a pretty dry remark.

Yosemite Sam: Did you know I was a weight-lifting champion?
Dusty Tails: I don't believe it.
Yosemite Sam: It's true! Last week I held up a train!

Kate: I don't know how Daffy can be such a perfect idiot.
Bugs: He practices a lot.

BUGS: Hey, Doc! Did you hear the joke about the ceiling?

DAFFY: No.

BUGS: Never mind. It's over your head.

DAFFY: What would I get if I poured boiling water down your rabbit hole?

BUGS: A hot, cross bunny!

DJ: At least those alien monsters are polite.

KATE: What makes you say that?

DJ: When they first saw us, they said, "Pleased to eat you!"

Q. Why isn't Marvin The Martian hungry after he's blasted into space?

A. He's just had a big launch!

DJ: I can't believe you know how to drive.

Daffy: Listen, bud — you can't expect a big star like me to *fly* south every winter.

Q. Why did Foghorn Leghorn cross the playground?
A. To get to the other slide!

Marvin The Martian: I'll see to it the earth comes to an end!

Daffy: That's impossible. The earth is round!

Bugs: Doc, I'm so tired, I can't even hop!

Daffy: Does that mean you're *out of bounds*?

Q. How does Bugs send his letters and packages?

A. By hare mail!

Q. What is Porky Pig's favorite ballet?

A. *Swine Lake.*

Daffy: Don't worry. No one ever starves in a desert.

Do: Why not?

Daffy: Because of all the sand which is here!

Do: Wow, Kate. After crawling through this cave, you're pretty dirty.

Kate: I'm even prettier when I'm clean.

Marvin The Martian: Could this be the height of stupidity?

Bugs: I don't know, Doc. How tall are you?

Q. Which alien monster has the best hearing?

A. The *eariest!*

BUGS: How do we keep those space monsters from charging?

DAFFY: Take away their credit cards?

DAFFY: If we're going to escape from Yosemite Sam, we better take showers.

DJ: What for?

DAFFY: So we can make a clean getaway!

Q. What did Marvin The Martian say when he landed in the flower bed?

A. "Take me to your weeder!"

BUGS: Daffy! You have a strange growth on your neck!

DAFFY: I do?

BUGS: Oh, my mistake. That's your head.

DAFFY: I happen to have one of those mighty minds!

BUGS: Yeah, Doc. Mighty empty.

DAFFY: I'm a real carefree duck.

DJ: You are?

DAFFY: Yep. I don't care, as long as it's free!

BUGS: Success hasn't gone to your head, Daffy.

DAFFY: Really?

BUGS: Yeah, just to your mouth!

DJ: I never gamble when I'm in Las Vegas.

DAFFY: Why not?

DJ: I even lose money on the postage stamp machines!

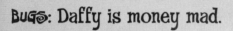

BUGS: Daffy is money mad.

KATE: Do tell.

BUGS: Yeah, he never has any money and that makes him mad.

KATE: Daffy, the studio is willing to pay you what you're worth.

DAFFY: It's about time.

KATE: Unfortunately, it's against the minimum wage laws.

Daffy: I'd go to the ends of the earth for fame and fortune.

Bugs: If only you'd stay there!

Q. Why did Yosemite Sam hide his loot in the freezer?

A. He wanted cold, hard cash.

Q. What did the judge yell when Pepe Le Pew walked in the courtroom?

A. Odor in the court!

Q. How do you know carrots are good for your eyes?

A. Have you ever seen Bugs Bunny wearing glasses?

Daffy: What kind of shoes should I wear to be a master spy?

Damian Drake: Sneakers.

Daffy: Why are you studying that book while we're in a flying car?

Bugs: I want a higher education!

Kate: Do rabbits use combs?

Bugs: No, we use *hare* brushes!

Q. What part of a computer does Marvin The Martian like best?

A. The space bar!

Q. How does Foghorn Leghorn stay fit?

A. He gets plenty of *eggs*ercise!

Q. Why is Bugs Bunny so cool?

A. He has a lot of fans!

Kate: Why are you carrying that car door through the desert?

Daffy: So when I get too hot, I can roll down the window!

Q. How do you make an alien monster float?

A. Two scoops of ice cream, root beer, and one alien monster!

Daffy: I wish I had enough money to buy a flying saucer.

Dd: What would you do with a flying saucer?

Daffy: Who wants a flying saucer? I just want the money!

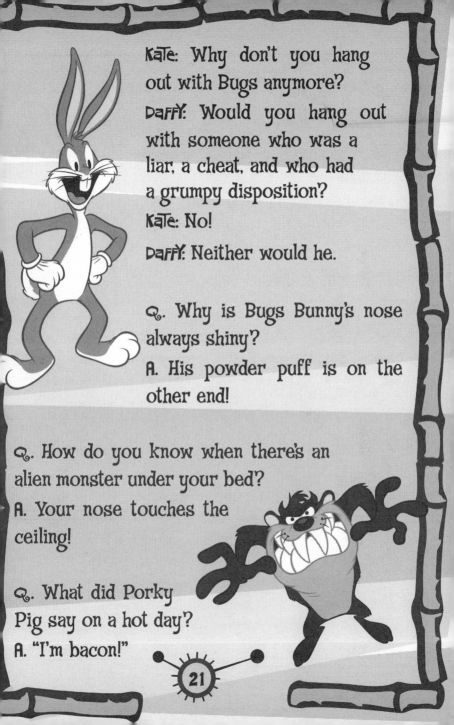

KATE: Why don't you hang out with Bugs anymore?

DAFFY: Would you hang out with someone who was a liar, a cheat, and who had a grumpy disposition?

KATE: No!

DAFFY: Neither would he.

Q. Why is Bugs Bunny's nose always shiny?

A. His powder puff is on the other end!

Q. How do you know when there's an alien monster under your bed?

A. Your nose touches the ceiling!

Q. What did Porky Pig say on a hot day?

A. "I'm bacon!"

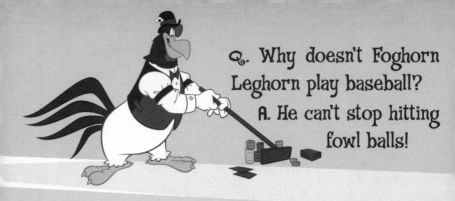

Q. Why doesn't Foghorn Leghorn play baseball?

A. He can't stop hitting fowl balls!

Q. On what does Marvin The Martian eat his supper?

A. Satellite dishes!

Q. What do you get from a two-headed alien monster?

A. Double talk!

Daffy: Haven't you ever seen me on TV?

Kate: On and off.

Daffy: How did you like me?

Kate: Off.

Q. How can you make Pepe Le Pew stop smelling?
A. Plug up his nose!

Q. What do alien monsters call Daffy when he's running away from them?
A. Fast food!

Q. What did Porky Pig say to Petunia about her scrambled eggs?
A. "That's all, yolks!"

Q. What do you use to paint Bugs Bunny's picture on a wall?
A. *Hare* spray!

Q. What's the best way to talk to the Tasmanian Devil?
A. Long distance!

KaTe: I hate caves! I don't want to get a disease from biting insects.

Bugs: Then don't bite any.

Daffy: You know what's going to be the hardest part about crashing our flying car?

Bugs: The ground?

Q. What do you get when you throw Daffy Duck into the ocean?

A. Saltwater Daffy!

Q. Why did Bugs Bunny get hit with a cream pie?

A. Because Daffy ducked!

Q. Where does Tweety like to go on vacation?

A. The Canary Islands!

Q. Where would Bugs go if he ever got married?

A. On his bunnymoon!

Q. What does Foghorn Leghorn say when he flirts with a hen?

A. "You must have been a beautiful egg!"

NASTY CANASTA: Why are you leaning on that banister?

YOSEMITE SAM: Because it's how I'm inclined!

KATE: Daffy, your speech was very moving.

DAFFY: Really?

KATE: Yes. I'm moving as far away from you as possible!

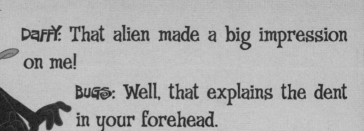

Daffy: That alien made a big impression on me!

Bugs: Well, that explains the dent in your forehead.

Daffy: Do you have change for a twenty-dollar bill?

Bugs: Sure, Daffy.

Daffy: Great! Then lend me ten bucks!

Tweety: How come you're such a good gardener, Granny?

Granny: I'm a down-to-earth person!

Tweety: Puddy-tat, if you want to chase me, it'll cost you three dollars.

Sylvester: Sheesh! So much for being as free as a bird!

Bugs: Daffy, nothing would please me more than to see you on TV.

Daffy: Really?

Bugs: Yeah. Then I could change channels!

Dd: I got my brains from my father.

Kate: Oh. Did he have any left over for himself?

Kate: Daffy, how would you like to travel to unknown places?

Daffy: You bet!

Kate: Great. Now get lost!

Q. Does Daffy Duck believe in love at first sight?

A. Only when he looks in the mirror!

YOSEMITE SAM: You're a mean, low-down, contemptible varmint!

COTTONTAIL SMITH: So?

YOSEMITE SAM: I knew we had a lot in common!

Q. Why did Damian Drake say, "1-2-3-4-5-6-7?"

A. He was a *counterspy*.

DAFFY: I'll have you know, one of my ancestors was a dentist who became President of the United States!

BUGS: Which one?

DAFFY: Mallard Fillmore.

Q. Is Pepe Le Pew spoiled?

A. No, he always smells like that!

KATE: You remind me of the ocean.

DAFFY: You mean romantic, wild, and restless?

KATE: No, you just make me sick.

EAU DE PHEW

BUGS: Daffy, you remind me of a cloudy day.

DAFFY: What makes you say that?

BUGS: Because the closest you'll ever come to a brainstorm is a light drizzle!

KATE: Did your mother ever lift weights?

DJ: No.

KATE: Then how did she raise a dumbbell like you?

NASTY CANASTA: How did you get away from those police dogs?

YOSEMITE SAM: I threw a penny down the alley and they followed the wrong cent!

Daffy: Why is DJ walking around the desert with a compass?

Bugs: He's trying to figure out if he's coming or going!

Daffy: Boy, I'm sure glad I wasn't born in France!

Bugs: Why not, Doc?

Daffy: I can't speak a word of French!

Q. On which side does Daffy have the most feathers?

A. The outside!

Q. When does it rain money in Las Vegas?

A. When there's some change in the weather!

Q. How does Bugs Bunny turn his soup to gold?

A. He puts in fourteen carrots!

Daffy: You can't eat me! I'm a famous movie and TV star!

Taz: Goodie! Taz was hoping for a ham sandwich!

Bugs: Daffy, I always thought you were meant to pilot a flying saucer.

Daffy: Why is that, Bugs, ol' pal?

Bugs: Because you take up space!

DoD: Thank goodness this jungle doesn't have lions.

Daffy: You got that right!

DoD: Yeah, the alligators scare them all away.

BUGS: Please don't fly this rocket car faster than the speed of sound.

DJ: Why not?

BUGS: I want to listen to the radio.

KATE: Why are you giving us the once-over?

TAZ: Me the jungle food inspector!

BUGS: Daffy, lying flat on your back won't make your problems go away.

DAFFY: On the contrary, things are looking up!

BUGS: Why are you leaving the studio?

DAFFY: The boss and I had a fight, and he wouldn't take back what he said.

BUGS: What did he say?

DAFFY: "You're fired!"

KATE: What did Taz say that scared you so much?

BUGS: He said he was going to get fed up with us soon!

KATE: The computer in this spy car will do half our work for us!

BUGS: Too bad the car doesn't have two computers.

DAFFY: Oh, I'm seeing spots before my eyes!

DOT: Have you seen a doctor?

DAFFY: No, just spots.

YOSEMITE SAM: I've made a small fortune in Las Vegas.

NASTY CANASTA: That's great, boss!

YOSEMITE SAM: Not really. I came here with a large fortune.

DAFFY: I'd like to see you in something long and flowing.

KATE: An evening gown?

DAFFY: I was thinking of the Mississippi River.

Q. How did Yosemite Sam's car happen to get into the casino?

A. He turned left at the buffet!

DAFFY: I'll get us out of this mess! All I have to do is use my head.

BUGS: I guess there's a first time for everything!

DJ: Go on, don't be shy. You can ask me out.

KaTe: Okay, get out.

DaFFY: I don't know the meaning of the word *fear*!

BUGS: Then again, you don't know the meaning of most words.

Q. What does Porky use to write with?

A. A pigpen!

Q. What do you call the tracks Bugs Bunny makes when he walks backward?

A. A receding *hare* line!

DJ: I learned how to make a campfire with only two sticks.

DaFFY: That's impressive.

DJ: Unfortunately, one of them was a matchstick.

Q. How does Foghorn Leghorn send his letters?

A. By *eggs*press mail!

Q. Why did Marvin The Martian get a ticket from Space Patrol?

A. He forgot to put a quarter in the parking meteor!

Q. What's black and white and stinks for just a second?

A. Pepe Le Pew going by on Rollerblades!

Q. How can you get Pepe Le Pew to stop smelling?

A. Cut off his nose!

KATE: Let me know if you spot any leopards.

DAFFY: Why should I? They already have spots.

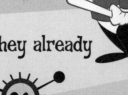

DAFFY: Looking at the dangers ahead, I get an empty feeling.

BUGS: Don't worry, Daffy. That empty feeling's just in your head.

ELMER FUDD: I'll have you know I've got a mind like a steel trap.

BUGS: Yeah, always closed!

DAFFY: What we need is a big cup of snew.

DJ: What's snew?

DAFFY: Not much. What's snew with you?

MR. WARNER: Your good ideas are like comets.

DAFFY: You mean they're glowing and brilliant?

MR. WARNER: No, they're very rare.

37

KATE: As a busy movie executive, do you ever have trouble making a decision?

MR. WARNER: Well, yes and no.

BUGS: Did you hear? I'm not going to eat carrots any longer.

KATE: Really?

BUGS: Yeah, the ones I eat are long enough!

ELMER FUDD: Gwacious! This is the ugliest picture in the entire museum!

BUGS: Hey, Fudsy, you're looking at a mirror.

KATE: Paris, France, sure is beautiful! Just look at that tower!

BUGS: It certainly is an eyeful.

KATE: Bugs, I hear you once fell through a theater floor.

BUGS: Eh, it was just a stage I was going through.

DAFFY: I hate jungles! I just got bitten by a gnatter baby!

KATE: What's a gnatter baby?

DAFFY: Nothing, sweetie. What's a gnatter with you?

Daffy: I never get tired of looking at myself in the mirror.

Bugs: I'm sure it's a shattering experience!

Q. Why did Taz have indigestion?

A. He ate someone who disagreed with him!

Kate: Boy, giraffes sure are tall!

Bugs: Yeah, but they don't eat much. After all, a little food goes a long way!

Q. Why didn't anyone know when Elmer Fudd bought a wig?

A. He kept it under his hat.

Q. Where does a one-ton Tweety sleep?
A. Anywhere he wants to!

Q. Why didn't Marvin The Martian like the amusement park on the moon?
A. It lacked atmosphere.

ELMER FUDD: How much is that wig?
TOUPEE SALESMAN: Twenty dollars plus tax.
ELMER FUDD: I'll take it, but forget the tacks. I'll use glue!

DAFFY: One day, every movie theater in the world will have my name up in lights!
BUGS: What are you going to do, change your name to "Exit"?

KATE: What's worse than a giraffe with a sore throat?

BUGS: A hippo with chapped lips!

KATE: Do you think Daffy responds to all the fan letters he gets?

BUGS: No. He hardly has time to write them all in the first place.

BUGS: Daffy, there's never a dull moment when you're around.

DAFFY: Really?

BUGS: Yeah, they're *all* dull!

42

YOSEMITE SAM: Every time I look at that gal Dusty Tails, I walk away with a big lump in my throat.

COTTONTAIL SMITH: Because she's so pretty?

YOSEMITE SAM: Because she's a karate expert!

KaTe: Do you think you could ever be happy with a girl like me?

DJ: Maybe, if she isn't *too* much like you.

Daffy: I'm good-looking, aren't I?

KaTe: In a way.

Daffy: In what way?

KaTe: Away off!

DAFFY: You haven't heard a word I've said!

BUGS: I'm listening to you. Didn't you see me yawning?

BUGS: You know the old saying about a person who needs no introduction?

DAFFY: Yeah?

BUGS: Well, you can use all the introductions you can get!

DAFFY: So you don't think my movie script is funny?

KATE: No, but when I threw it into the furnace, the fire roared!

YOSEMITE SAM: How can one hombre make so many mistakes in a single day?

COTTONTAIL SMITH: I get up early.

DAFFY: What do you think of my movie script? Give me your honest opinion.

MR. WARNER: It's worthless!

DAFFY: I know, but tell me anyway.

BUGS: Kate and DJ make a perfect couple, don't you think?

DAFFY: I'll say! He's a pill and she's a headache!

Daffy: Which way did Elmer go?

Bugs: He's 'round in front.

Daffy: I know what he looks like, I wanted to know where he went!

Bugs: Wow, Daffy! Your last scene had the audience in the aisles!

Daffy: Laughing?

Bugs: Yawning and stretching.

Daffy: I'll have you know I get letters from ladies in every city I visit.

Bugs: Landladies, no doubt.

YOSEMITE SAM: The law is coming! Quick, jump out that-there window!

NASTY CANASTA: But we're on the thirteenth floor!

YOSEMITE SAM: This ain't no time to be superstitious!

Kate: Daffy sure is temperamental.

Bugs: Yeah, ninety percent temper and ten percent mental.

Kate: Has anyone ever told you how wonderful you are?

DD: No.

Kate: Then where did you get the idea?

Daffy: I lost my job because of illness and fatigue.

DD: That's not what I heard.

Daffy: It's true! Mr. Warner said he was sick and tired of me.

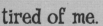

Q. If athletes get athlete's foot and farmers get corns, what does Marvin The Martian get?

A. *Missiletoe!*

GRANNY: Sylvester is so smart he even has his own computer.

DJ: Does he use it much?

GRANNY: Well, he likes to chase the mouse.

Q. What's the difference between counterfeit bills and Bugs when he's angry?

A. One is bad money and the other is a mad bunny!

Q. When Bugs passes through Albuquerque, what's the headline in the newspaper?

A. HARE TODAY – GONE TOMORROW!

Dd: How did you get all those bruises?

Daffy: The studio executives threw a loud party downstairs.

Dd: So?

Daffy: I was the loud party!

DJ: We've got a flat tire!

DAFFY: It must have been that fork in the road.

KATE: Did you know that women are smarter than men?

DJ: No, I didn't.

KATE: See what I mean?

DAFFY: Show me a tough guy and I'll show you a coward.

YOSEMITE SAM: Well, I'm a tough guy!

DAFFY: And I'm a coward.

Bugs: You can't eat me, Taz. I'm a comedian.

Taz: So?

Bugs: I taste funny!

Daffy: We can't get too lost. I have this map of the desert!

Bugs: I hate to break it to you, Daffy, but that's sandpaper.

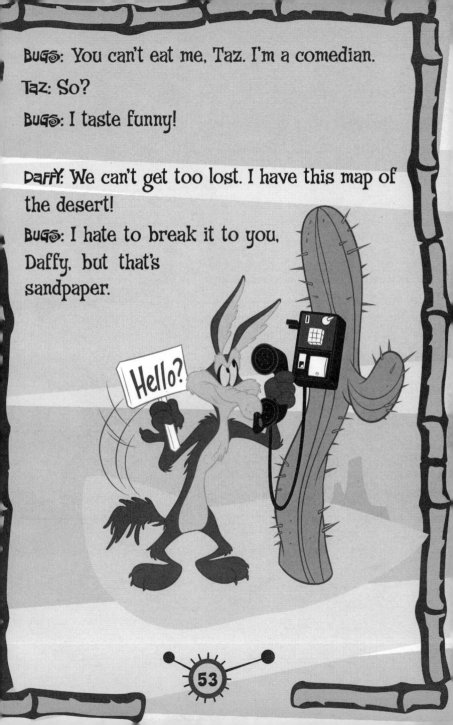

Hello?

Daffy: Why do you keep honking the car horn?

DJ: To keep the elephants away.

Daffy: That's ridiculous! There isn't an elephant around for a thousand miles!

DJ: See, it works.

Daffy: I suggest we have a battle of wits!

Bugs: Personally, I think you're low on ammunition.

Daffy: What do you mean? I'm a great wit!

Bugs: Well, you're half right.

Elmer Fudd: So you think I'm stupid, eh? You'll be sorry!

Bugs: I've always been sorry you're stupid.

AREA 52 SCIENTIST: I can make a clone of anything.

DAFFY: Here's ten bucks! Double my money!

DAFFY: Does this movie have a happy ending?

BUGS: Well, I'll be glad when your scenes are over!